Poppleton

Read more
Poppleton
books!

Poppleton

Written by Newbery Medalist
CYNTHIA RYLANT

Illustrated by
MARK TEAGUE

ACORN™
SCHOLASTIC INC.

Library of Congress Cataloging-in-Publication Data

Names: Rylant, Cynthia, author. | Teague, Mark, illustrator. | Rylant, Cynthia. Poppleton ; 1.
Title: Poppleton / written by Newbery Medalist Cynthia Rylant ; illustrated by Mark Teague.
Description: [New edition]. | New York : Acorn/Scholastic Inc., [2019] | Series: Poppleton ; 1
Originally published: New York : Blue Sky Press, 1997. | Summary: Poppleton the pig moves from the city to a small town, where he makes new friends and spends Mondays reading adventure books in the library.
Identifiers: LCCN 2018055965| ISBN 9781338566673 (pb) | ISBN 9781338566680 (hc) | ISBN 9781338566796 (ebk)
Subjects: LCSH: Poppleton (Fictitious character) — Juvenile fiction. | Swine — Juvenile fiction. | Friendship — Juvenile fiction. | Books and reading — Juvenile fiction. | CYAC: Pigs — Fiction. | Friendship — Fiction. | Books and reading — Fiction.
Classification: LCC PZ7.R982 Po 2019 | DDC 813.54 [E] — dc23
LC record available at https://lccn.loc.gov/2018055965

10 9 8 7 6 5 4 3 2 1   19 20 21 22 23

Printed in China   62
This edition first printing, September 2019
Book design by Maria Mercado

CONTENTS

MEET THE CHARACTERS

Poppleton

Cherry Sue

Fillmore

NEIGHBORS

Poppleton used to be a city pig.
He did city things.
He took taxis.
He jogged in the park.
He went to museums.

Then one day Poppleton
got tired of city life.

He moved to a small house
in a small town.

Poppleton's small house
was charming.

It had a little sunroom
where Poppleton took naps.

It had lots and lots of shelves
where Poppleton kept things.

It had a little garden
where Poppleton planted corn.

And it had Cherry Sue.
Cherry Sue was Poppleton's
new neighbor.

Cherry Sue was very friendly.

In the mornings she called out,
"Yoo-hoo! Poppleton!
Would you like some oatmeal?"

So Poppleton had oatmeal
with Cherry Sue.

In the afternoons she called out,
"Yoo-hoo! Poppleton!
Would you like a toasted cheese?"

So Poppleton had toasted cheese
with Cherry Sue.

At night she called out,
"Yoo-hoo! Poppleton!
Would you like spaghetti?"

So Poppleton had spaghetti
with Cherry Sue.

This went on day after day.

At first it was fun.
But not for long.

Some mornings Poppleton did not
want oatmeal.
He wanted to sleep.

Some afternoons Poppleton did not
want toasted cheese.
He wanted TV.

Some nights Poppleton did not
want spaghetti.
He wanted to practice
playing his harmonica.

But Cherry Sue kept calling,
"Yoo-hoo! Poppleton!"

One day when he was watering his lawn,
Poppleton couldn't take it anymore.

When Cherry Sue stuck her head out
the window and yelled "Yoo-hoo!"
Poppleton soaked her with the hose.

"Poppleton!" cried Cherry Sue, dripping.

Poppleton felt awful.

He ran to get a towel for Cherry Sue.

"I'm sorry, Cherry Sue,"
said Poppleton.
"I just got so sick of oatmeal
and toasted cheese and spaghetti.
Sometimes I just like to be alone."

"You too?" said Cherry Sue.
"I kept inviting you over because
I didn't know how to **stop** inviting you over.
I thought it might hurt your feelings."

Then Poppleton soaked **himself**
with the hose.

They laughed and laughed.

Poppleton and Cherry Sue
were best friends from then on.

THE LIBRARY

Poppleton went to the library
every Monday.
Monday was **always** Poppleton's
library day.

If Cherry Sue invited him
to tea on Monday,
Poppleton would say,
"Sorry. Library day."

If there was a wonderful parade
in town on Monday,
Poppleton would say,
"Too bad. Library day."

Poppleton took library day
very seriously.

At the library Poppleton always
got a table all to himself.

He spread out each of his things
on the table:
his eyeglasses, his tissues,
his lip balm, his pocket watch,
his book marker, and his duffel.

Then he began to read.

Poppleton liked adventure stories.
He buried his head
in an adventure book every Monday,
and left it there all day long.

Sometimes he needed
a tissue for a sad part.

Sometimes he needed
lip balm for a dry part.

Sometimes he needed
his pocket watch for a slow part.

But he loved his adventure.

At the end of the day,
Poppleton finished the story.

He thanked the librarian
and packed up his things in his duffel.

Then he slowly walked home,
all dreamy from so much adventure.

Monday was Poppleton's
favorite day of all.

THE PILL

Poppleton's friend Fillmore
was sick in bed.

Poppleton brought Fillmore
some chicken soup.

"I feel terrible, Poppleton,"
said Fillmore.

"Have a bowl of soup," said Poppleton.

"First I have to take my pill,"
said Fillmore.

"Where is it?" asked Poppleton.

"Over there on the table," said Fillmore.

Poppleton brought Fillmore his pill.

"I can't take it like that," said Fillmore.
"You have to hide it."

"Hide it?" asked Poppleton.

"You have to hide it in my food," said Fillmore.

"I'll put it in the soup," said Poppleton.

"No, it has to be in something sweet," said Fillmore.

"Sweet?" asked Poppleton.

"Sweet and soft," said Fillmore.

"Sweet and soft?" asked Poppleton.

"Sweet and soft with raspberry filling," said Fillmore.

"Sweet and soft with raspberry filling?"
asked Poppleton.

"And chocolate on top," said Fillmore.

"Chocolate on…
Fillmore, are you talking about
Cherry Sue's Heavenly Cake?"
asked Poppleton.

Fillmore smiled.

Poppleton went away.

Soon he came back with
Cherry Sue's Heavenly Cake.

"Now I can hide your pill,"
said Poppleton.

"Don't tell me which piece of cake it's in,"
said Fillmore.

Poppleton sliced the cake into ten pieces.

He hid Fillmore's pill in one of them.

Fillmore had the first piece.

"Yum," said Fillmore.
"Did I take my pill?"

Poppleton shook his head.

Fillmore had another piece.

"Yum," said Fillmore. "Did I take it?"

Poppleton shook his head.

Fillmore ate piece after piece after piece. "Did I take it?"

Poppleton kept shaking his head.

Finally there was only one piece of cake left.

"Thank goodness," said Poppleton.

Fillmore looked at the piece of cake.

"I can't eat that one," he said.
"It has a pill."

"WELL, WHAT CAN YOU EAT?"
shouted Poppleton.

"Something lemony," said Fillmore.
"With coconut."

"I feel sick," said Poppleton.
"Move over."

Poppleton and Fillmore were sick in bed
for three days.

They took **lots** of pills.
It took twenty-seven cakes
to get them down.

ABOUT THE CREATORS

CYNTHIA RYLANT

has written more than one hundred books, including *Dog Heaven*, *Cat Heaven*, and the Newbery Medal–winning novel *Missing May*. She lives with her pets in Oregon.

MARK TEAGUE

lives in New York State with his family, which includes a dog and two cats, but no pigs, llamas, or goats, and only an occasional mouse. Mark is the author of many books and the illustrator of many more, including the How Do Dinosaurs series.

YOU CAN DRAW

1. Draw an egg lightly with a pencil. (You will erase most of this as you go along!)

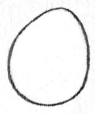

2. Add ovals for arms and legs — no details yet, just get the basic shapes.

3. Make a circle for Poppleton's head, with a smaller circle for his snout. (See? You're already erasing part of your egg!)

4. Add triangle shapes for ears and make a shirt.

POPPLETON!

5. He's a happy pig! Add a smile! (You need to erase part of your circle to do this.)

6. Finish Poppleton's face with eyes and nostrils.

7. Don't forget his hoofs and tail! That's Poppleton!

8. Color in your drawing!

WHAT'S YOUR STORY?

Poppleton loves to read adventure stories.
Imagine **you** and Poppleton are on an adventure.
Where would your adventure take place?
What would you do?
Write and draw your story!